ROUND TRIP
ANN JONAS

SCHOLASTIC INC.
New York Toronto London Auckland Sydney

ISBN 0-590-40956-5

12 11 10 9 8 7 6 5 4 3 2 1   6 7 8 9/8 01 2/9

Printed in the U.S.A.   08

For Don Nina Amy

We started out as soon as it was light.

Our neighborhood was quiet, the houses dark.
The sun shone on the pond.

and soon saw our moonlit street.

Town was empty,
the stores still closed.

We passed a small farm in the valley,

We passed smoky factories.

and fields of wheat.
We counted the cars on a train.

It rained hard
and puddles formed.

The road wound through the mountains.
Trails led into the woods.

Lightning flashed across the sky.

On the highway,
we headed for the coast.

We went under an expressway.

The water was rough, the waves high.

As the smoke from the fireworks drifted away
and the birds resettled in the trees, we drove on.

We followed the shore past marshy inlets
and summer cottages.

We saw fireworks and stopped to watch.

Then we saw the city.

We looked back. Searchlights pierced the sky.

We crossed a bridge,

In the country, telephone poles lined the road.

and we were there.

We left the shining, starlit city.

After parking the car, we rode the subway.

and picked up our car from the garage.

Then we went to a movie.

Then we had dinner in a restaurant,

and to the top of the tallest building.
We looked down.

Back on the street,
we looked up at where we had been.